A Sky Full of Stars

by Judy Kentor Schmauss

Houghton Mifflin Harcourt.

PHOTOGRAPHY CREDITS: COVER (bg) ©Moodboard/Alamy Images; 3 (b) ©Image Work/amanaimagesRF/Getty Images; 4 (b) ©Photodisc/Getty Images; 5 (t) ©Gerard Lodriguss/Photo Researchers, Inc./Getty Images; 7 (l) ©Ocean/Corbis; (r) ©Duncan Smith/Photodisc/Getty Images; 8 (t) ©Image Work/amanaimagesRF/Getty Images; 9 (b) ©Gerard Lodriguss/Photo Researchers/Getty Images; 10 (t) ©Project with vigour/Aflo Foto Agency/Alamy Images; 12 (b) ©Lawrence Migdale/Photo Researchers/Getty Images; 13 (t) ©StockTrek/Photodisc/Getty Images; 14 (b) Courtesy, NASA

Printed in the U.S.A.

ISBN: 978-0-544-07331-9

13 14 15 16 17 18 19 20 1083 20 19 18

4500710511   B C D E F G

Contents

Vocabulary	Stretch Vocabulary	
constellation	navigate	refracting
orbit	celestial	reflecting

Introduction

Look up at the sky on a clear night. You will see an entire sky filled with twinkling points of light. Look a little more closely to find some shapes among the stars. Does that group of stars look like a lion? What about the group of stars to the left? A bear?

When you look for lions and other shapes among the stars, you are looking for constellations. Constellations are groups of stars that look like animals, objects, or characters from a story. They're like a connect-the-dots game in the sky! We've given them names, both common and scientific, as a way to talk about them.

Let's explore the pictures in the sky.

This constellation is named after Cassiopeia, the queen of Ethiopia.

Constellations and Cultures

There are many cultures around the world with stories and myths about the constellations. Each culture has its own views and explanations.

Many constellations contain clusters of stars. In the constellation called Taurus (the Bull), separate clusters make up the bull's different body parts. One of the clusters is the Pleiades. Although the Pleiades consists of hundreds of stars, you can see only seven of them without a telescope.

According to Greek mythology, the Pleiades—the seven daughters of Atlas and Pleione—were chased for seven years by a hunter named Orion. Zeus changed Orion into a constellation and the sisters into stars.

The Pleiades, also called the Seven Sisters, are one of the closest star clusters to Earth. They are in the constellation of Taurus.

the Big Dipper in the northern sky

Stars that make up the constellation Orion represent different forms in different cultures. In early Mesopotamia, the stars that make up Orion were seen as a shepherd. The Inuit, a Native American people, thought the three stars in Orion's belt looked like seal hunters. The Egyptians believed that the constellation was a falcon-headed god named Horus. They saw Horus riding in a boat.

The Big Dipper is part of another constellation, called Ursa Major. According to Native American folklore, a bear can be seen in the four stars that make up the bowl part of the dipper. The three stars in the handle are three hunters chasing the bear.

Before and during the Civil War, enslaved people who wanted to escape used the Big Dipper to point them north to freedom. The song "Follow the Drinking Gourd" was written and used as a guide by those who were traveling on the Underground Railroad. The "drinking gourd" is the Big Dipper.

Steering by the Stars

The word *navigate* means "to find your way from one place to another." Today, we navigate using a GPS (Global Positioning System) in our cars or use online maps on our phones or computers. However, in ancient times, sailors used the sun, moon, and stars to navigate. This kind of navigation is called celestial navigation.

As Earth orbits the sun, the part of the sky that we can see at night changes. Because the stars don't move, but we do, it makes sense that if you watched the night sky every night for a few weeks or a month, you would see different stars and constellations.

If you were on a ship, you could use the stars to determine where you started and the direction in which you were going. Depending on which constellations and stars you saw on your journey, you'd know where you were. In other words, if you knew that a constellation could only be seen from the Northern Hemisphere and you didn't see it, you'd know that you were really lost!

In order to use celestial navigation to figure out where they were and in which direction to travel, ancient sailors, or mariners, relied on an instrument called an astrolabe.

An astrolabe is used to determine the altitude, or height above sea level, of stars and constellations. An astrolabe works like a small metal map of the night sky. By rotating the parts to the current date, time, and latitude, ancient sailors could tell where their ship was.

Modern sailors who still prefer to sail by celestial navigation now use sextants to help them. A sextant measures how high the sun is in the sky during the day. It's part telescope and part mirror. It can also measure how high the moon and stars are at night.

early mariner's astrolabe

modern sextant

To find the constellation Orion in the winter sky, look for the three close-together stars that make up Orion's Belt.

Wonderful Winter Constellations

Certain constellations are visible in the Northern Hemisphere only in the winter. These include Orion, Canis Major, Gemini, Perseus, and Taurus.

Orion is the Hunter. This constellation is the brightest and most distinct constellation in the winter sky.

Canis Major is also known as the Great Dog. According to Greek mythology, Canis Major is one of Orion's hunting dogs. It contains the brightest star in the sky and is easiest to see between November and March.

Gemini is a well-known constellation. It is often referred to as the Twins. You can see the Twins holding hands in the sky.

Perseus is the hero who saved the king and queen's daughter and defeated Cetus. He also saved his people from Medusa, who could turn people to stone if they looked at her face. The constellation shows Perseus with his arm outstretched, battling Cetus.

Taurus is the Bull. The Greeks thought that Taurus was Zeus disguised as a white bull. On Taurus's shoulder sits the Pleiades—the seven daughters of Atlas and Pleione. You can see Taurus in the night sky between November and March.

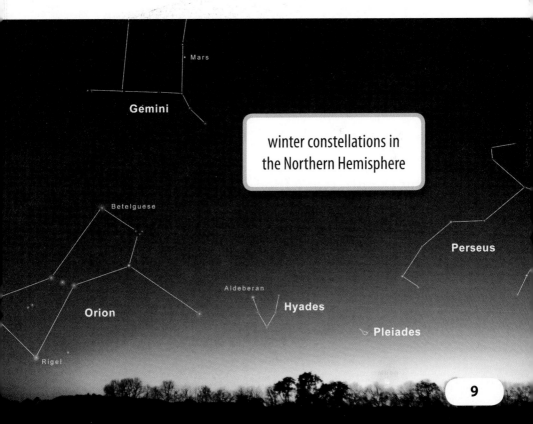

Mars

Gemini

winter constellations in the Northern Hemisphere

Betelguese

Perseus

Orion

Aldeberan

Hyades

Pleiades

Rigel

Scenes in the Summer Sky

Summer brings a whole new list of characters to the drama in the sky. They include Aquila, Cygnus, Hercules, Lyra, Ophiuchus, Sagittarius, and Scorpius.

Aquila is the Celestial Eagle, the servant of Zeus. He kept Zeus's thunderbolts handy and ran Zeus's errands. A straight line of three stars makes up part of Aquila's wing. In certain cultures in India, the three stars are said to be the footprints of a great man.

The constellations Cygnus (above) and Aquila are visible in the summer nighttime sky from this beach in Hawaii.

Cygnus is known as the Swan or the Northern Cross. In some mythology, Cygnus was a friend of the son of Apollo. When Apollo's son fell into the Eridanus River, Cygnus tried to save him. Zeus then turned Cygnus into a swan.

Hercules is the kneeling Greek warrior in the sky. He was victorious over other constellations such as Leo (the Lion), Hydra (the Nine-Headed Serpent), and Draco (the Dragon).

Lyra is the fifth-brightest star in the sky. Also known as the Lyre, it is a small harp, which is a musical instrument. Each April, meteors burst out of Lyra in what's known as the Lyrid Meteor Shower.

Ophiuchus is the Serpent Bearer. It can be seen from June through October and looks somewhat like a teapot. According to Greek mythology, Ophiuchus was a great healer. Zeus was angry with him but then later honored him by putting him in the sky.

Sagittarius is known as the Centaur, a creature that was half man and half horse. He was a skilled hunter and an artist. He is said to be aiming a bow at his neighbor Scorpius. Zeus put Sagittarius in the sky because of his artistic talents, rather than for his ability to hunt.

Scorpius is the Scorpion. Scorpius is one of the largest and brightest star clusters in the sky. You can see Scorpius crawling close to the horizon in the southern part of the sky. The scorpion once had claws, but they were removed to form the constellation Libra.

Tools for Viewing

Telescopes are the best tools you can use to view the stars. They come in many sizes, from small home versions to the powerful scopes found at universities and observatories.

An eyeglass maker invented the first telescope in the early 1600s. Galileo Galilei, an Italian astronomer, perfected the telescope by using a series of lenses. His telescope allowed him to magnify an object to 30 times its size.

There are two types of modern telescopes. A refracting telescope uses lenses, much like the original version. A reflecting telescope uses a series of mirrors that are positioned in a way that bounces the light around and magnifies the object. Some telescopes, especially the larger ones in observatories, use a combination of lenses and mirrors.

The Hale Telescope at Mount Palomar Observatory in California is a reflecting telescope. It was once the world's largest telescope.

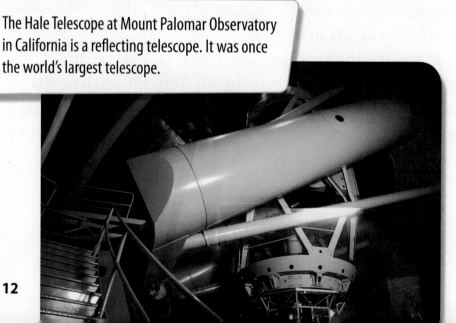

The initial plans for the Hubble Space Telescope were begun in 1975. Congress approved the funds in 1977.

Currently, the largest and most powerful telescope is the Hubble Space Telescope. Hubble is an observatory that was carried into space by the *Discovery* space shuttle in 1990 and continues to orbit Earth. Hubble is a reflecting telescope and directs the light from stars and other objects into several instruments, including a camera. The camera then sends the pictures to scientists on Earth.

Hubble works well because of where it is placed. Because the atmosphere around Earth is full of different gases, Hubble was purposely positioned about 595 kilometers (km), or 370 miles (mi), above Earth. Outside Earth's atmosphere, Hubble is able to record very clear images that are more detailed and accurate than those taken by other telescopes. Hubble has supplied thousands of astronomers on Earth with data they could not get in any other way.

What's Next

Hubble is likely to remain in orbit until the James Webb Space Telescope (JWST) takes its place. NASA plans to launch the JWST in 2018.

Originally called the "Next Generation Space Telescope," or NGST, the JWST improves upon the technology used in Hubble. The JWST will have a 6.5 meter (21 feet) mirror and a sun shield that's about as large as a tennis court. When the telescope is launched, the pieces will be folded up. They will unfold when the telescope reaches its planned orbit about 1.5 million km (1 million miles) from Earth. The JWST will use mainly infrared technology to gather data and take pictures of the galaxies that are farthest away—and therefore the oldest. For years, the JWST will provide vital information to thousands of earthbound astronomers.

our galaxy, the Milky Way

Make a Data Table

Research the constellations that you can see from your location during the current season. Identify the major stars within the constellations, and create a chart that compares their location, size, scientific name, common name, and other relevant information.

Write a Report

Astronomers and astrophysicists study the planets and stars. Research an astronomer or an astrophysicist. Find out where the scientist works, what the scientist does, and any important discoveries that he or she has made. Write a report that includes the facts you found. Share your report with your class.

Glossary

celestial [suh·LES·chuhl] Belonging or relating to the sky.

constellation [kahn·stuh·LAY·shuhn] A pattern of stars that forms an imaginary picture or design in the sky.

navigate [NAV·ih·gayt] To plan or direct the route or course of a ship, aircraft, or other form of transportation.

orbit [AWR·bit] The path of one object in space around another object.

reflecting [rih·FLEKT·ing] Throwing light or energy back from a surface.

refracting [rih·FRAKT·ing] Bending or changing the direction of light.